Wild Words

Volume 1

The Carrick-on-Shannon Children's Literature Festival is a collective endeavour developed with the support of Leitrim County Council Arts Office, The Reading Room, Leitrim Library Service, The Dock and Carrick Cineplex.

While most events during the festival are designed for young readers, *Wild Words* is a special programme for young people between thirteen and eighteen years who have moved on to writing short stories and poetry themselves.

This publication and the Carrick-on-Shannon Children's Literature Festival are made possible with the financial support of Leitrim County Council, The Arts Council and Children's Books Ireland.

A collection of writing by young people produced in association with the Carrick-on-Shannon Children's Literature Festival.

Published by Leitrim County Council Arts Office

Leitrim County Council Arts Office,

Aras an Chontae,

Carrick-on-Shannon,

Co. Leitrim,

Ireland.

00353 7196 21694

www.leitrimarts.ie

ISBN: 978-0-9576189-1-6

Editorial Panel:
Helen Carr, Anna Carey, Philip Delamere, Avril Carr.

Foreword

By Helen Carr

When Leitrim County Council put out a call for writing submissions from teenagers for inclusion in *Wild Words* they were pleasantly surprised to receive so many entries of such a high quality, across a range of subject matters and styles and from such a variety of age groups and geographic locations.

Selecting the pieces for inclusion in *Wild Words* has been very interesting and rewarding. It was difficult to narrow all the submissions down to the eighteen that made the final cut, but it had to be done. There is such a broad range of maturity in the thirteen to eighteen age group and it's wonderful to witness so many writers moving towards greater mastery of their craft. All these young writers are bridging the gap from childhood to adulthood and it's not a linear process; teenagers will sometimes feel more like the children they were only recently, while at other times they feel like adults who should be in charge of their own lives. We can see these conflicting feelings in many of the writings in this collection – in the stories, the lyrics and the poetry.

What we were looking for in this collection were strong storylines and ideas, credible characters and high-quality writing. We found all this, and also we found a love of language and words, and a striving to employ them to express emotions accurately, describe scenes or capture feelings. Several themes came up more than once – the harking back to childhood, the frustration of being a teenager or of living up to others' expectations, dealing with loss, and the need to look beyond first impressions were strong themes throughout the collection. The importance of books and music to teenagers can also be seen in the inclusion of rap and song lyrics, and in the two stories inspired by J.D. Salinger's *The Catcher in the Rye*.

Whether fantasy, satire, poetry, love story or gritty realism, all the selected writings have something to say to young people today.

Welcome to *Wild Words*. Read and enjoy!

Helen Carr

July 2013

Contents

Humans

By Aidan Black, age 16.

When I was young my people were a hopeful race. The future looked so bright back then. The last war had ended in my grandfather's time. Somehow we all started listening to each other; reason became the basis for all opinions. Knowledge marched forward, the gods stepped back, and we began to dream of travelling to the stars.

But then they came, those that were already travelling among the stars, they came here in their steel ships and talked in our tongue. They seemed to know all of our language and culture; our wise asked them how. They spoke of watching us from afar and learning our ways. They asked us if they could set up a place upon the planet: a 'Knowledge Embassy'. A place where any could go to ask them any question in the hope that they knew the answer; where we could go to ask for help, if we wanted it. And our wise rejoiced in the knowledge that they were wise enough to only offer help when we needed it and not when we wanted it. Our fears that they may be a pompous race that believed themselves superior and/or capable of understanding our needs were quelled and we agreed to their proposal.

But we were betrayed. When they returned they came with weapons of destruction and turned us into slaves. They made us work in giant mines that they slowly made more automatic. They processed what they brought up in giant machines and dumped most of it randomly around the lands creating vast mountains of junk and polluting half the lakes and rivers. A tiny amount of what we (and their automated monstrosities) mined was shipped off the planet. Only a few of us were even allowed to get food for the rest of us. And then they kept that food under lock and key refusing to feed those that would not work. But as the mines became more automated they needed fewer of us, and they only fed those of us that they needed. We began to starve.

I somehow managed to live to be old. I was a quick learner and they managed to teach me how to fix the automated monstrosities so

I was useful to them long after I was too frail for manual labour. Then when I fell sick people smuggled me food in exchange for tales of the old world. I made it my mission to keep the image of what we were alive in the minds of the young.

Then it happened. One day when I was giving my final talk to the kids that were going to be taken for work the next month, a spaceship landed off schedule. This had never happened before. Most ships landed at very regular times bringing supplies for the humans or taking away the rare minerals we had mined. Any landing outside of that was always small and the landing area was always cleared in advance. This one was a surprise even for the humans.

This ship was larger than any I had ever seen before. It could house an entire army, and as I would soon find out, it did. First, a unit of twenty-one humans came out and started off towards the so-called 'Knowledge Embassy'. Then the army began to show itself. It was a wonder to watch, within forty seconds an army 100,000 strong along with a thousand giant machines of destruction was deployed and ready for battle.

As the twenty-one humans reached the building, the doors swung open for them. Just over two minutes later the occupants of the building were marched out hands bound. Quickly afterwards a similar procedure was carried out with all the buildings. Another group was then sent out to each building to pick up military supplies. A large group was also sent to shut off the machines and round up the supervisors. Once all the humans and weapons were safely away, the army retracted into the ship, a procedure that only took slightly longer than deployment: about fifty-five seconds.

Then there was only one human left and they began to speak. Somehow their voice was heard equally all over the island.

'There is nothing we could say that could even be the beginning of the most inadequate apology. Know however that those who did this to you will never be free again. We are here to help now; we will strive never to let this happen to you or anyone else ever again. We will give you all the aid you want in the restoration of your civilisation and your planet. When the material that was taken becomes valuable to you we will return it a thousand fold. We hope that one day you can come to forgive us, to blame the individuals and not the group. I wish there were words for how sorry I am. Please know that what you have seen of us is the worst of us, most of us are not this bad.'

I turn to the kids I had been speaking to.

'Mark those words well my children. Just as you should never judge an individual by their group, you should never judge a group by a small number of its individuals. The little hope we had has become great, go my children, reforge this world, I must rest.'

He never woke from that sleep.

Effie and the Mysterious Village

By Chelsea Bright, age 13.

The grass is normally green here but today, it is not. I wish I wasn't so obsessed with little changes around my tree but I am. Hello, my name is Effie. I am an orphaned daughter of a woodcutter. It was a long time ago now. 7 years, I am 13 now, I think, somewhere around that age anyway. I don't remember my parents, if that's what you call those people who take care of you when you're small and have to be fed by spoon. Yes, I live in a small pine tree in a forest on my own. I have the last things my father had with him when he left. I don't know where he is. I can't remember anything about him. I have to go out everyday and find fish or nuts. I watch the fish from the small stream near a field of bluebells from behind and POUNCE!! I catch it in the river. I've just come back from looking for food. I got a hoard of blackberries and two fish. The sun is beginning to set and I hear wolves beginning to howl at the harvest moon. I shiver. It's cold tonight and once again I have no blankets. I climb to the thickest branch and fix myself. I give a loud yawn.

I suddenly feel a rush of warm air. What is going on? I open my blue eyes. Straight in front of me is a round tent. Have the Comanche got me? I shake off the blankets I never had and rush outside. There are people, of different types. Boys are wearing velvet cloths and are selling garments, spices and many other delicacies. I feel exhilarant. Women are washing and cleaning and young girls of my age are setting out a big square with stalls. There must be a special thing going on this evening. Someone catches my hand and pulls me back into the tent. It is a man, he is tall, with black-cropped hair and brown eyes, and he is tanned. 'Who are you?' he asks, his voice very low. 'I am Effie,' I begin 'where am I and who are you?' The man leads me outside. 'Well Effie, My name is Samson, and you are in the village of Lakendell,' he says to me. I look him up and down. 'Do you want to give me and my sons a hand with the stalls?' I nod happily but I add, 'Do I get anything out of it?' Samson chuckled, 'What do you mean?' He asked. 'Can I get some food afterwards?' Samson considered. 'Okay,' he eventually answered. Samson leads me over to a stall selling gems. Two boys are standing there and they wave. I wave back and take my place behind the stall. One of the boys winks at me. He comes over and introduces himself. 'Hello, my name is André' He was very shy. Samson gives me an hourglass and tells me when it has been turned over my shift is finished. I take a box of Zircon and Sapphires and held them out for the crowds to see.

Afterwards when the hourglass was turned, Samson gave me a pat on the back. I got a leg of a chicken. I walked away from the store, quite happy with myself when André ran over and patted me on the shoulder. I nearly jumped out of my skin. André produced a lovely stone gem in my favourite colour, blue. 'This is an aquamarine stone gem that is on its own chain,' André produced the blue chain, also aquamarine. 'It's really nice, André.' I said. André put the gem on the chain and gave it to me. He turned back and waved once again.

I walked down the long brown path. It was beginning to get dark when I saw a woman outside a pink velvet tent. The tent was for fortune telling and other things. The woman called out to me. 'Want a reading?' I didn't understand what she meant, but I strolled into the tent anyway.

Inside, were a chair and a small wooden table with a black crystal ball. The woman sat across from me. 'Close your eyes,' She began. 'My name is Marabella, and I am about to reveal all the mysteries you would like solved.' I closed my eyes tightly. I began to see green pastures and Lakendell came into view. 'Your mother was a young seamstress, the best in Lakendell and your father was a woodcutter, and they met at the funeral of the Mayor, and began courtship. On your mother's twenty-first birthday she fell pregnant with a daughter, who she named,' Marabella paused and I answered, 'Effie.' 'Yes, your mother was not approved of by her family and ran away with your father. Your mother's name was Alena and your father's Andrew. Andrew Mc Flamel. They fled with you to the forests of America. The rumours had spread too great in their homeland, rumours that your mother was an Enchantress and your father was a Wizard. Most believed this to be a long old tale of bored women. But they were not wrong. Your mother was born with a curse, to live

13

the life of a monster. When you were born, your mother fled, for her own selfish reasons. She returned to Lakendell, bearing the features of a creature long gone from this world. She was captured and kept in a cell. Your father then began experimenting, and from his disguise, he dumped you in a field of bluebells, your mother's favourite part of the forest. He grew mad with grief, and has never been found. You will live long and prosper my child. Your time is coming. You wield powers that have been unknown since the Pleistocene era. Effie, believe in yourself and remember this, you will return soon, to the life your mythical family once had. You will save them, but you must wait until I call you.'

I asked. 'Who are you, Marabella?'

She told me to open my eyes and it was day once again, dawn in fact, and I was lying face down in the field of Bluebells. I stood up and saw the aquamarine necklace. A tall woman who looked just like me. Blonde hair and teal eyes. She wore an amethyst-coloured dress. She bowed and spoke 'Effie, you have grown so much.' So we walked into the wilderness and I felt overjoyed to see my mother, Alena, once more.

Emma Lyons

By Annie Eliza Brown, age 13.

An old, wrinkly woman sat down in front of the children in the class. 'Tell us a story!' they pleaded. 'The one about how you became a faerie! Pretty please!' She smiled and took a deep breath, then began to tell the most amazing story I'd ever heard.

'As soon as I came within range of the forest, I suddenly felt very sick, and had a throbbing pain in my back. I continued on towards the oak tree in the centre of the forest, the pain increasing with every step I took. My footfalls became slower and more strained as I got nearer and nearer to the tree, until I couldn't go any further, still at least ten feet away from the tree.

I still didn't know why I had been drawn to the tree, as if there was a string connecting the trunk to my body that was pulling me closer. With every inch nearer I got, the more the pain coursed around inside me. It was like a song that my ears strained to hear, but the more I heard, the more it hurt. As I lay on the ground, unable to go closer although my heart ached to, the pain in my back stopped for a moment. Then I could slowly feel the skin of my back painlessly separating to make room for two gigantic things to unfold. I looked over my shoulder and saw two amazing blue wings fluttering and realized with a jolt that they were my wings! All the sick feelings had stopped and I felt like the tree was welcoming me, like I could finally hear its song without hurting. I looked down into a puddle, and the reflection I saw wasn't what I was expecting at all… There was a blue tinge to my skin, and my hair had grown longer and wavy. My ears had become a little pointed at the top and my features were altogether much sharper. Yet what astonished me the most was the deep emerald green that I saw in my own eyes, not the usual muddy brown colour that I saw in the mirror every morning, but these clear, shining, inquisitive eyes that stared back at me made me jump.

'Hello.' I heard a voice say. I looked up from staring into the puddle and saw a girl with long black hair hovering beside me, her

15

wings fluttering, making her look incredible. 'Come with me,' she said, 'and we'll explain this situation to you.' She smiled and held out her hand. I took hold of her green-tinted hand and I flew with her to the tree. I don't know how I knew how to use my wings without being clumsy, but I glided seamlessly through the air alongside this other girl. 'You're a faerie now,' she began, as we landed at the trunk of the oak. 'Most likely, some of your family were faeries, but sometimes it can skip generations and generations before a new faerie is born!' she said with a chuckle. Wait a minute, I thought. Me? Emma Lyons? A faerie? This is truly impossible! She brought me in to a village of sorts through a gap in the trunk of the tree. 'I'm Elinor. What's your name, might I ask?' she said, interrupting my train of thought. I stumbled across words to finally stutter 'Emma Lyons', but as soon as Elinor heard my name, she took to squealing and flitting about with excitement. 'Another Lyons!' she called. 'Oh, we haven't seen one of you for years! The day has finally come that we are graced by the magnificent Lyons family once again!' and with that she curtseyed to me. It would have been an understatement to say I was gobsmacked. A crowd had begun to gather and I could hear them mutter things like 'Is it true? We've finally got another Lyons?' and 'She does look like them, doesn't she?'

A male faerie fluttered towards me and everyone hushed to hear what he had to say. 'I am Titan, the leader of this whole village,' he said. 'You really are a Lyons… Your family were the most powerful faeries ever, and the faerie gene has skipped countless generations in your family. But we finally have you here with us – and with that, I introduce your instructor, Elinor.' Elinor looked like she had just won the lottery. 'She will take you to your house.' Elinor suddenly grabbed my arm and we flew off at high speed towards a small cottage.

'This is where you live now, Emma,' she said, opening the door and leading me inside. 'Put these on,' she said, handing me a bundle of clothes that looked like they were made out of a flower display. 'You'll really feel like a faerie then, and you'll look the part! Your room is just through there.' she directed me to a cosy bedroom with a four-poster bed and a dressing table, and a wardrobe that was covering the whole back wall! I examined the clothes more closely, and found that they actually were made of flower petals and leaves. I put on the dress and looked in the mirror, and thought it was the most fabulous dress I had ever seen. I went back out to Elinor and she surveyed me quickly. 'You're gorgeous!' she exclaimed. I really felt gorgeous too. Suddenly the telephone rang. I didn't think faeries could use technology… Elinor motioned for me to answer. 'It's your house!' she chirped. I picked up the phone and before I could even say hello, a cruel voice said:

'I hear there's a Lyons back. Well don't think you'll be staying too long, because I'm after you. I finished off the last one, and you're next! Your family isn't magnificent or amazing or wonderful, you're just liars.' and they promptly hung up. I put down the phone, in a state of shock. It had been shocking enough, having just found out I was a faerie, but now some stranger was out to get me! I quickly told Elinor what had happened, and she stood up and ushered me out the door. 'Oh dear!' she said, sounding flustered. 'We really should have expected this, considering what happened to the last Lyons,' she pulled me along as she kept talking. 'We must get you to Titan at once!' she said, worriedly. I hesitantly asked her about the last Lyons. 'Well,' she said, 'He didn't live for long. William Lyons was his name. He was a faerie that never knew right from wrong, even if he didn't mean any harm. Yet, somehow, he caused harm to someone, because he was killed, and the murderer was never found.' I gasped, because I suddenly realized how much danger I was in. Elinor took me in to where Titan lived, and told me to wait in the hall. The house was so ornately decorated, and as I looked around in amazement, I could hear worried voices getting higher and higher.

'Emma,' I heard Titan's voice say. 'Come in please.' I slowly creaked open the door and stepped inside. Elinor was standing beside Titan, who was sitting behind an antique desk and frowning. 'We have decided that for your safety, you move to another village. You must leave now. Elinor will bring you there. You're going to a place where you'll never be found. And Emma, I'm afraid you can't come back here.' I nodded at this, mainly because I had no words. Elinor nodded to Titan, and brought me away.

After two hours of flying, we landed in a tiny, dilapidated village. Elinor led me to another cottage, which was my new home. We sat for a while, discussing what had happened, but eventually we got up to explore the village.

There were only a few other faeries living in the village, and as we met and spoke to each one, a certain thing became very clear- they wanted us to help rebuild the village.'

The old woman laughed and said, 'And, I suppose that is why you're all here today!' The children gazed up at her, amazed at what she had just told them. 'Did you really make the village good again?' they asked innocently. She nodded and said 'With the help of Elinor of course.' Suddenly a shrill bell sounded throughout the school, signalling the end of the day. The students gathered up their things, and flitted off in different directions towards their parents, as I strolled away, thinking about what an amazing life Emma Lyons had.

Perfect Imperfection

By Anna Ceroni, age 16.

There are few feelings more irritating than the light, ticklish flick of your knee-length skirt against the back of your legs. Combine that with the aggravating clip-clop sound of those ridiculously childish patent leather shoes against the footpath and that aroma that's possibly a mix of car fumes and burning rubber, and it's perfectly obvious why I was walking home from school with such an intense scowl on my face. There were other contributing factors of course, but for the moment I'll stick with those that can be classified as environmental.

The whole scene was ridiculously suburban. The roads were lined on both sides with never-ending rows of terraced houses, the glossy pavements were scattered with leaves from the irritatingly symmetrical trees, and then there was me, walking homewards in my immaculate school uniform with hair fixed neatly out of place, the very definition of middle class.

Damn. I could feel the soft fabric of my knee-socks sliding down my leg. I crouched down by a garden wall and yanked them back up to knees once more. I got up from the ground, straightening myself out, only to lift my head and meet the all too familiar eyes of one Freddy Blake.

He smiled at me. Well, the word 'smile,' in this case, is a severe understatement. His mouth contorted and stretched itself into this ridiculous, semi-circular arc of delight, his entire expression engulfed by this monstrosity. I nodded politely at him, deciding not to give him the satisfaction of seeing me smile back in return.

'Hi there,' he grinned, straightening his blazer. 'Coincidental isn't it, that we meet so often here?'

Hardly coincidental, I thought, exasperatedly. You're clearly some kind of determined stalker. Yet I decided to be polite, knowing that the importance put on being polite to so respectable a ¬¬boy carried much more weight than any slight strain on my patience.

'I suppose it is,' I murmured, trying my best not to drift into my usual monotone, which would so quickly let him know how little I cared for him.

He beamed back at me as if I had just declared my undying love for him, rather than just muttering some quiet agreement.

'Can I carry your books?' he offered pleasantly.

'If you so wish,' I replied, knowing that this in turn entailed his walking me home.

He scooped up the pile of books I'd left on the ground almost effortlessly, a strength that could probably be attributed to his involvement in multiple sports teams. Freddy was every mother's wet dream, and, inclusively, my own mother's wet dream. Polite, respectable, sporty and vaguely attractive, Freddy was everything I'd been led to believe a boy should be. Many a girl would be pleased to be in my position, delighted to have him as their obedient stalker and pursuer. Yet I was harshly indifferent.

We walked down the path together, Freddy still beaming and carrying my books, making attempts at conversation. I became passive, agreeing with most everything he uttered. Yes, the weather was miserable, yes, I was so glad Christmas term was almost over, yes, it is a shame we don't go to the same school, yes, I suppose it would be rather odd if we did… On and on it went, until I found myself contemplating whether or not humans had a sort of auto-pilot function, whereby this incessant agreeing and nodding could just be done purely without effort, rigid and robot-like.

We took a turn down Holly Court, Freddy seeming worryingly confident in his direction. I decided not to ponder too much about how on earth he happened to know where I lived. He turned to me once more, that almost painful-looking smile still gracing his face.

'You're awfully quiet, Emma,' he said, his eyes scanning my face in an attempt to meet my gaze.

My thoughts turned momentarily harsh and sarcastic and I desperately wanted to make some remark about the human habit of stating the obvious. Yet he was too pleasant to be truly snide to, so I tried to make up for my sour thoughts and to attempt friendliness.

'Well then, it's a good thing you're so talkative,' I replied, flashing him what could have been almost a hint of a smile.

'Yeah, I suppose we're a good combination,' he said, grinning even more widely than before, if that were indeed possible.

I felt like I wanted to throw something at him, that dustbin over there, perhaps. How I ached to wrench it off the ground and fling it right over Freddy and his ridiculous smile. The whole situation was just so cheesy, so awful, predictable and cliché.

Perfect Emma, perfect girl, perfect Freddy, perfect boy. The whole thing was just one awful, obnoxious perfection.

We arrived in front of the white-painted gate bordering my house. Freddy stopped in his tracks and turned to face me. He handed me my books, and after hesitating slightly, beamed at me once more.

'See you around, then,' he said cordially. It was a statement rather than a question. His confidence was both charming and irritating, though more so the latter, really.

My eyes flicked to the first floor window of my house, through which I could see my mother staring outside at us with a look of obvious approval. Even from here I could smell the very delight on her breath. I resolved not to give my mother any more fuel for her glee.

'Bye, then,' I replied. 'See you soon.'

I waved goodbye to him, and taking care not to be too eager in my departure, shifted slowly around the gate and into my front garden. Freddy flashed me a parting smile and sauntered off in the opposite direction. Just a moment too late, my mother appeared on the doorstep, demanding to know everything and calling enthusiastically after the departed Freddy.

'Darling, was that Freddy I saw you with? Such a charming lad. Would he not come in for a bit? Stay for dinner? A cup of tea, even?' She blurred all her words together with the coherency of an excited twelve-year-old girl who'd just found out that she'd acquired tickets to see her favourite boy-band. I don't think I mattered to her in the slightest in that moment. I was simply a daughter, a purely functional being, her doll and pet, to be groomed, polished and admired from afar. She cared only about the concept of me, about maintaining my perfection and being able to take pride in me, for I was, so to speak, an accomplishment of hers.

I pushed past her, up the stairs and lay down on my bed. My eyes shut and I willed yet another day to draw to a close.

***

The changing room smelled distinctly like a combination of old socks and cheap cosmetics. The whole room was terrifyingly pink, pink walls, pink lockers, pink shower tiles and pink window frames. Not to mention the pink blush of the bare skin which the girls displayed without much reservation. I could hear the snap of pastel bra straps, the crisp, musical giggles that erupted from the girls and the pop of the caps being removed from various cans of deodorant. Such was the sound of femininity.

I was awkwardness incarnate. I hid in a corner, trying not to let my eyes drift from my own activity, but yet, letting them all the same.

My eyes flicked to the opposite wall. There, tall, slim and undeniably gorgeous, stood Jude Owens, fiddling with the shoelaces on her trainers. I knew such staring was every kind of detestable perverted; yet I had not the will to turn away. She flicked her shampoo-advert hair onto her shoulders, displaying her long, elegant neck. My eyes traced the outline of it, its porcelain quality, with sweet, delicate collarbones poking up like folds of white icing. A spattering of freckles lay across her midriff and travelled right across her shoulders and …

I forced my eyes shut, disgusted at myself. Yet my lack of self control meant that within minutes I was looking back at her once more. She stood up straight and I felt my insides collapse as she stretched, showing every curve in her figure to advantage. She turned around and I immediately fixed my eyes elsewhere. Then I looked back at her again briefly, only to spot her tongue flicking across her lips, both tempting and tormenting me.

I turned my back to her, and buried my eyes in my gym bag, wanting to scream, cry and throw up, all at once. The fact she enticed me was dangerous, terrifyingly so. I was Emma, perfection itself, destined for a life of being inoffensive, intended for clean-cut, charming and suitably masculine Freddy Blake. Perfection was not satisfying, but it was also uncomplicated, and I knew that submitting to the allure of Jude Owens would be complication itself.

I felt two light taps on my shoulder. I turned around, my eyes meeting with those of several girls in my class.

'I saw you walking home with Freddy Blake yesterday,' one girl giggled, her glittery lips extended in a smile. 'You two are so perfect.'

I half-smiled in response, but said nothing. The other girls nodded enthusiastically in agreement. Their sounds of their delighted giggles rose like balloons, with an elation so alien to me.

'You're playing in the Christmas concert on Friday, aren't you Emma?' offered another, perhaps sensing my discomfort. I nodded, slowly, too shy to look her in the eye.

'I heard the boys from St Paul's are coming,' added another girl, 'Freddy will get to see you play!'

At this, I gagged, and my desire to retch was almost overpowering. It was all too ideal, sweet Emma to play the piano faultlessly, with her dearest Freddy watching her and waiting for her afterwards, no doubt with a bunch of flowers.

I edged slowly away from the other girls, staring at my feet so intensely that they blurred into giant flippers. I wished to be anywhere and everywhere but there, to be anything or anyone but myself, to have any life but mine with its disgusting perfection.

***

Wooden floors have always made me uncomfortable. Well, maybe not always, but they certainly did just then as I stared at the floor, studying the wood with ridiculous intensity. The plonk of old piano keys and a slightly off-key choir buzzed in the background. The staring helped me distance myself from the scene, for I knew otherwise I would have already acquired multiple headaches from the lively rehearsing around me. Teachers bustled around, ostensibly in a tizzy with the prospect of tomorrow's concert.

After some time, the choir were commanded to cease their singing, and the elderly music teacher shifted her figure from the piano stool. I knew this was my cue. I practically tiptoed towards the piano, so afraid was I of marking the floor with my shoes. Well, truthfully, a combination of that, and natural timidity and diffidence.

I perched on the edge of the piano stool, adjusting my figure to suit the position of my feet in relation to the pedal. One of the teachers produced sheet music, which I knew I would barely glance at, but which also felt comforting, like a kind of insurance.

It was then that I began, my fingers touching each key with an easy familiarity, producing the ruthlessly overplayed first movement of Beethoven's Moonlight Sonata. Without a waver, without a falter, without a blunder I played my performance utterly faultless.

I produced the final chords and then lifted my fingers slowly from the keys, letting them hover momentarily over the piano before putting my hands by my sides once more. Some of the girls standing around clapped supportively, and I quickly got up and walked back to my previous seat, so as not to allow time for myself to start blushing.

I spotted Jude Owens, detached from the crowd, her head buried in her own sheet music. My gaze caught hers, and she smiled and approached me.

'You were just … Wow,' she said, earnestly, 'I pity the act following you.'

Her tone was sweet, soft and genuine. I could barely catch her words, so captivated was I with her very being. She smiled at me and her lips curved so perfectly, so invitingly, two dimples emerging on her freckled cheeks. My words caught in the back of my throat. I had words, yet, I didn't. All possible coherence was lost once I met her eyes.

'Thanks,' I murmured so quietly I doubted she'd heard, but she seemed to guess what I was attempting to say anyway, and nodded in response.

'I'm so nervous,' she confessed, 'I've never played in front of a crowd. I'm so afraid my violin will fly out of my hands and knock out someone in the audience.'

I felt obliged to laugh, but my hesitancy made it sound much more like a cough than anything else. She edged closer to me, seemingly to try and hear what I was saying. Her dainty breaths were warm against the back of my ear. Her figure brushed softly against my shoulder, sending strange electric pulses down my arm. She smelled wonderful, like a mixture of vanilla and summer flowers. I was drowning in the moment, up to my neck in it, way out of my depth. She pulled back slightly and I relaxed, my breath gushing out in a stream of sighs.

I felt completely enticed by something I'd sworn not to allow myself to have. I could feel my wall of resistance dismantling, a crack forming in the faultless brickwork.

***

All I could ever recall about past Christmas concerts was the sheer piercing loudness of them, this year being no exception. The audience were small blotches on a dim background, the only proper light in the hall being the large overly bright and almost invasive spotlights, which peered down on the performers from atop the stage ceiling. I peeked through a slit in the curtain material. The choir's song was drawing to a close.

'Emma Jones?'

I heard my name being whispered from somewhere behind me. I turned around, only to see someone holding out a small, red rose towards me.

'It's from Freddy,' said the figure, following up this statement with a suggestive wink, 'he says, break a leg.'

I held back what could have been either tears or vomit. What was once nervousness then turned to a feeling of wretchedness. He seemed to follow me everywhere. I didn't hate him per se, but I loathed the concept of him. I hated that he was apparently so perfect for me, when, in truth, he was the furthest thing possible from it.

I crouched in a ball on the ground and held in my tears. I couldn't cry, I wouldn't cry. But as with many things I couldn't do, I wanted to, rather desperately.

I heard the choir's song end on a slightly shaky note and knew this was my cue. Once they'd cleared the way, I stepped out onto the stage, letting my nervous feet guide me to the piano. I pushed every concern to the back of my mind and put fingers to keys.

Within minutes I could hear impressed gasps resonating through the audience, little echoing ripples of expressive breath spreading through the crowd. Had I been properly aware at the time, I imagine I may have felt some sense of pride or achievement. Yet I focussed only on a figure at the wing of the stage, Jude Owens, who looked positively serene and was staring solely at me, plain, and ordinary me, sitting so awkwardly on the little piano stool.

I'll never know quite what happened in that moment. I must have just broken. I had been a vase, perched precariously on the edge of a wobbly, short-legged table. It was the inevitable.

My fingers, which had been so perfectly in control, so exact and fine in their playing, seemed to droop clumsily and I played every wrong chord imaginable. F-sharps happened where they shouldn't have, my fingers tripped over themselves, trying to cling desperately to what had been initially so faultless.

It was then that I surrendered. I dropped my hands by my sides, swallowed any reluctance I'd ever had and got up from the piano stool. I just stood there, staring blankly ahead. I hardly knew what I was doing or what I was thinking, but I felt strangely liberated. I'd messed up this performance so much that I felt nothing I could do could make it any worse. I felt no embarrassment. I could just stand there, free from concern.

I wanted to make mistakes, now that I'd made several so painlessly. Not everything I did was perfect, and now everyone knew it.

Now there was one mistake in particular I wanted to make.

I walked slowly towards the wing of the stage, wrapped my arms around the beautiful Jude Owens and kissed her slowly on the lips.

Perhaps I was on fire; that's what one usually experiences with such events. Yet I can't describe it properly. I know only that I felt free, gloriously so. Consequences didn't matter anymore. I wasn't perfect. I was magnificently imperfect. And being imperfect felt more perfect than anything in my life ever had.

Adaptation

By Paul Clifford (Young Melee), age 15.

I say rules are made to be broken,

not said to be spoken

Whenever someone does something crazy cos they feel they need to be noticed.

When I say this I don't mean to be hopeless,

But the future's going nowhere it's got to a standstill.

So I'm just trying to make music and trying to get more fans in.

It's mad when everyday,

when we open our mouths gotta watch what we say.

We have to think twice.

I'm telling you live don't think, cos you can't live twice.

Got one life, make sure you live right.

Cos when you've no life left, hope you've lived it to fullest – be like Dappy no regrets.

Develop your identity.

A unique individual is what you're meant to be.

I'm not talking bout when you're in a shop and they ask to see I.D.

Cos that just gets electrical D.I.D.

I'm talking bout your identity as a human being

And what's usually seen

from your points of view

And what you do.

Cos it all reflects on you.

You say you didn't know, but I bet you do.

I'm on a continuous beat, but you're trying to mess the loop.

I got more problems, but the mess is new.

I'm seeing changes like pac,

So I've got to adapt.

My pockets are malnourished I'm trying to make them fat.

I'm trying to make the ching ching from these raps.

Why lie when there's proof?

You can save from a lie you can't save from the truth.

You get the mic and get brave in the booth.

I'm brave all the time, it's just some of my lyrics get saved for the booth.

My Poem

By Meadbh Donohoe, age 17.

You walk through the forest,
It's a deep brown warm colour, an orange yellow
And brown blanket of leaves lie beneath you.
Where you walk, makes a fresh crunchy sound.
The dark grey water, waves gush with the wind.
You feel carefree.
It's beautiful.

The Dark

By Eimear Gallagher, age 16.

I am alone.

The light is fading.

Darkness creeps in as a blanket of shadows.

No one to help me escape.

I am alone.

Light shines in the dark, but

there's no light to lead me to safety.

I'm surrounded by nightmares.

I am alone.

Nothing will be left of me.

Everything I know has disappeared.

All beauty is gone.

I am alone.

Nowhere to go.

The stars have faded away.

The dark has taken over me.

Hazle Weatherfield and the Mystery of the Stolen Cookies

By Phoebe Caulfield (aka Josh McLaren), age 17.

Hazle Weatherfield was nothing short of a genius. Only sixteen years old and already a world-renowned detective. Well, maybe not world-renowned, but at least a few people knew about her and she had been in the paper a couple of times. So it was a bit of a shock when the very wealthy, very upper class Old Lady Hayward, who could have hired the whole of Scotland Yard if she felt like it, invited Hazle to her splendid home to present her with a new case. Hazle felt slightly out of place in her casual grey clothes as she sat on the bright white leather couch.

'So they stole your cookies,' Hazle asked writing down notes in her notebook.

'No,' answered Old Lady Hayward, 'they stole my treasured golden necklace.'

'Did you see anything particularly odd on the night in question?' asked Hazle breaking out the staple detective questions.

'Of course not' replied OLH in her high-pitched rich lady voice. She signalled with her hand for Hazle to come closer. Hazle leaned slightly towards the matching couch that OLH was sitting on. 'Is it true you were…' whispered OLH '…an orphan?' Hazle was sick of rich, snobby people thinking she could not be a detective because she was an orphan, she didn't mind if they were ageist or sexist, but being orphanist really drove her mad.

'Yes, that piece of scandalous gossip is correct' Hazle confirmed. OLH resigned to thinking for a few seconds and then quickly shook her head and took a sip of tea from her delicate china mug. Hazle frowned into her own cup full of Earl Grey and tried to take a tiny sip but slurped it so loudly that it probably caused an earthquake in Brazil or somewhere.

'So these thieves stole your necklace and cookies?' Hazle asked.

'Yes,' replied OLH. 'The boobs.'

'And what were these cookies like?' Hazle poised to take notes.

'Shouldn't we talk about the necklace first?' asked OLH.

'Excuse me Miss, but I am the detective here,' announced Hazle, reminding OLH because she was clearly a little senile.

'Okay then … ' said OLH, 'well they were chocolate chip and almond…home baked…………by me of course'

'Mrs Hayward,' shouted the maid from the kitchen, 'I just finished baking the cookies.'

Hazle gave OLH the stare that said 'You're a liar' because OLH was clearly a liar. 'Okay. And the necklace?' asked Hazle, trying to cover up an awkward pause.

'It was solid gold and was studded with diamonds that spelled out the words Party Animal,' answered OLH. 'It's rumoured my great, great grandmother stole it from Tupac.'

'Ok Miss,' said Hazle, going to leave because she was bored. 'I'll find the people who stole your necklace…if there's nothing good on telly.'

'Why, thank you so much,' said OLH as she quickly escorted Hazle out the door.

***

Hazle sat a park bench; she had received a note from a mysterious person asking her to meet them here. Normally that would have been dangerous but she had brought her crossbow, which was sitting on the bench beside her, so she felt safe enough.

'Hello, Hazle,' said a deep voice behind her.

'Ugh!' yelled Hazle and collapsed onto the ground 'Just leave me alone.' She looked at the shiny red cowboy boots in front of her; she slowly looked up to see her father's smiling face looking down at her.

'Still as dramatic as ever?' her father asked laughing.

'How would you know, Dad?' asked Hazle. 'You haven't seen me in around sixteen years.' Her father smiled and sat down on the bench.

'Still got the old family crossbow I see,' he commented picking up the crossbow and examining it.

Yes!' shouted Hazle snatching it out of his hands. 'What are you even doing here, Dad?'

'Just came to reconnect with the child I abandoned leaving her extremely emotionally damaged,' said Hudson wiping a speck of dust off his fancy suit. 'Oh, and I just solved that case you were hired for.'

'What?!' shouted Hazle jumping up. 'I only left that place like twenty minutes ago.'

'Yeah, I'm pretty good at this whole detective malarkey,' smiled Hudson crossing his legs, which made the sun shine on his shiny boots.

'Nobody could solve a case that quickly,' said Hazle reasonably.

'Well I can,' smiled Hudson blind to his daughter's distress. 'It was the gardener,' he finished throwing down a file that he produced from his suit. Hazle grabbed it and roughly ripped it open. She looked at the picture inside and had to admit that the guy looked like a thief.

'How's your mother these days?' asked Hudson watching Hazle reading the file.

'She's dead, Dad!' Hazle replied softly.

'Oh, when did that happen?' asked Hudson sounding uninterested.

'Probably around two days after I was born,' Hazle reminded him, 'she was executed because she was a serial killer.'

'Oh yeah,' smiled Hudson, 'I forgot about all that.'

'How could you forget?' shouted Hazle angrily. 'It's the part of my back story that made me want to become a detective; it's on my blog for frack sake.'

'Oh, I never know what's going to set you off,' laughed Hudson like it was a joke. 'Well, see ya, kiddo,' he said, standing up on the bench and doing a back flip.

Hazle grunted and sat down and started reading the file.

'I don't know, Noelle,' Hazle moaned rubbing her eyes. 'Like maybe he is guilty.'

'Well he sure looks like he is,' said Noelle taking a pull of her cigarette and blowing the smoke into Hazle's face. Hazle coughed and waved the smoke away and took a bit of the Big Mac she had ordered.

'I don't think you're meant to be smoking inside,' Hazle reminded Noelle.

'Whatever,' answered Noelle, 'I've become a vegetarian.'

'Are you sure?' asked Hazle as she watched Noelle take a bit out of her triple Big Mac with extra bacon. 'Burgers are mostly made of beef...well they used to be.'

'In case you haven't noticed,' argued Noelle, 'these burgers have lettuce in them you boob.'

Hazle frowned at Noelle and looked at the baby shoes Noelle was wearing as she took another puff from her cigarette.

'So, he probably is guilty but I just have a feeling in my gut that he isn't,' said Hazle. 'Or maybe it's just nausea from seeing my Dad.'

'Maybe you should stop being so self-absorbed and think about others for a while, preferably me,' Noelle replied.

'Oh my Allah!' gasped Hazle as she noticed something on the file. 'Dad!' Hazle shouted. She was standing in the middle of a large park gripping onto the file. 'Dad!' she yelled again at thin air.

'You shrieked,' she heard a smooth voice reply behind her.

'Dad, the gardener couldn't have done it,' Hazle explained.

'Excuse me?' asked Hudson rubbing a speck of dirt off his shiny boots.

'The gardener did not steal the necklace,' Hazle said excitedly.

'What makes you say that?' asked Hudson.

'In this file it says he's allergic to all kinds of nuts and OLH said that the thief ate all her homemade cookies,' Hazle explained quickly, 'so the gardener could not have done it.'

'Maybe the thief didn't eat the cookies,' countered Hudson. 'Maybe OLH did and just didn't want to seem fat.'

'Listen dad, I know I hate you and you have no reason, but just trust me on this little thing. Think of it as payback for sixteen years of emotional anguish,' Hazle pleaded.

'OK,' Hudson answered.

'What, just OK?' Hazle asked slightly shocked.

'Yeah, I discovered the old cookie thing as well. I just wanted to see if you could figure it out,' Hudson smiled. 'That emotional anguish served you well.'

'Do you know who did do it then?' Hazle asked confused.

'Oh yes,' Hudson smiled back tapping his coat pocket. 'Let's just say Berger knows…'

***

'So OLH, it seems as if you lied to me,' said Hudson, 'and my daughter.'

'Whatever do you mean,' replied OLH, pretending like she did not know.

'You said your necklace was stolen,' replied Hudson.

'Which it indeed was,' said OLH, trying to hide something.

'Tell me Hazle,' said Hudson turning to her on the white couch they were sitting on, 'if I had a cookie and I took that cookie, would the cookie be stolen?'

'No … ?' replied Hazle confused.

'Exactly,' exclaimed Hudson. 'Unless I suffer from multiple personality disorder I still have the cookie therefore it is not stolen.'

'What is this poppycock about?' asked OLH.

'What my father's convoluted story is trying to express is that nobody stole your necklace as you took your own necklace and hid it.'

'Why would I do something like that?' replied OLH, clearly guilty of the crime.

'Because just last week,' answered Hudson, 'you took out a new insurance policy with the company Berger and Co.' Hudson then produced a copy of an insurance document 'Is that your signature there?' asked Hudson.

'Yes it is,' confirmed OLH. 'But lots of people take out insurance.'

'Yes, but you only insured the necklace in question,' retorted Hudson, 'and it seems that if the necklace does get stolen you get a very large payment.'

'I still have no idea what you are babbling on about,' said OLH feigning ignorance.

'Listen lady,' said Hazle standing up, 'you hid the necklace said it was stolen, hired me so I would never find out you stole it, plant evidence on the gardener and get the cash, the end.'

'Oh frack,' replied OLH.

Based on events in The Catcher in the Rye.

Surviving the Storm

By Megan Melia, age 15.

It was the early morning of 26 September 2012. I was woken with a start by the sound of the house phone ringing in the hall. In a haze I wondered if it would be left to me to retrieve it, I looked at my phone it was 6.30am. I heard my mother answer it quietly in her sleepy state, still groggy. I rolled over back into the groove in my pillow; although curious, I was happy that I did not have to leave the warmth and security of my blankets. As soon as I heard 'hello Ann' I darted straight upright in bed, I flashed back to the same morning a year before to the same news 'who?' An ecstasy of thoughts whirled in my head. I ran to my parent's room, my mum's face told me all I needed to know she said 'Jack's gone'. Tears began to swell in my eyes and stream down my face, salty tears mixed in with the sleep stung my tired eyes. A sea of emotion, and I was drowning.

The morning was a rush. A call to my aunt Rita. A return of emotions. Realising I had no appropriate clothes, Mum and I went to our local clothes shop. A shop assistant, a friend of my mother's commented on my tear-stained face and offered condolences. I couldn't bear to believe this was reality. The car journey to their house was intolerable, it rained and rained, it pelted against my windows, and the storm reflected in my eyes, I didn't know if I could survive it. I had to be strong.

Upon arrival my cousin's dog Rosie met us, she knew just as well as we did that it was a devastating occasion we had come for. Inside I met my broken cousins. First Ben in the same suit he had buried his father in. I nearly knocked him with the force of my newly-formed grief as I hugged him, his hand full of hair gel, busying himself. Then John, usually loud and cheeky, forced into silence. Chris distraught, then Emily helping her mother make tea. The only thing I could say was 'sorry'.

People called as word travelled around. It was a solemn day, it flashed by even though at the time I thought it would never be over, the closer to the eye of the storm we came. At home it was 9.30pm, tomorrow we would see him. I washed my hair and went to bed.

The next day was a Wednesday; we travelled up again returning to the same sadness. We sat around waiting for organisation, then followed John and Ben in John's car to the morgue. There we met the rest of our family and the other family of theirs. As I said my silent words in my mind next to his coffin, I put a small teddy bear inside the silk covering; he did not look the same. He looked more mature than his seventeen years. I clutched my father's hand and as we took turns saying prayers I thought it silly that my father could not remember all the words and I gave him a few helpful pushes. We followed the hearse home. We met other cars which waited for us to pass. We watched as he was carried to the blue boxroom. There were many cards on the table, with a vase of white lilies. They stood for so much that day. The smell of a burning candle added to our emotions.

The next day I wore black clothes. We got there early as Emily had asked me and my brother to do a prayer. I prepared it for the time I would need it. I cried into my father's already sodden jacket as they closed the door for their last precious moments together. I cried until I could not see past the storm in my eyes. They came out; emotions flooded the hall like a tsunami. We walked united out of the house. My father and brother helped to carry the coffin up to the top of their lane. We followed close behind their cars. Upon arriving at the church we waited for the throngs of people to get inside, but there were too many to fit in. I carried flowers and set them around the pew at the front. Another flash back to the same church a year ago, at Jack's fathers mass when I did the same thing.

The mass ended and everyone journeyed to the final resting place, next to his father. The rain stopped after the ceremony, was the storm ending? I waited by my cousin Ben's side as he wept by the grave. I then left him to mourn alone. In a hall the neighbours had organised tea, the aftermath of the storm was to be seen in the flooded grass patches. I let my tea go cold and salty with tears, but I knew he was in a better place now. I was happy for him.

A few weeks passed, and we had returned to the same place to say new prayers at my cousin Emily's wedding. The storm was rough, and we remember it well, but I have survived and shall never forget it.

Fear Dubh

By Mollie Miller, age 15.

As my eyelids slowly drooped, falling into sleep, I started to feel more alive.

Running through the fields beyond his house, basking in the suns golden rays. More alive than life itself. Bliss. And then wading in the small bubbling stream.

The tiny fish suspiciously inspecting my toes. Darting, scared if I wiggled them. And the rain gently fell, coating my hair with its tiny droplets. The pure serenity of being here, near where he lived, before…well before what happened. Funny how I always have such peaceful dreams but quick as anything they change tack.

The lightning comes, the thunder rebounds around the hills, the rain pelts down. All of a sudden he would be there, out of my reach, screaming once more. Calling for help. But I couldn't. If the thing saw me it would take me too, that I was sure of. So I crouched behind a boulder, filled with a sense of foreboding. With one final scream I saw the thing, as tall as anything and wearing a pin-stripped suit. The only feature I could never recreate in my dreams was his face. It was left black. A white oval on top of his spindly body. He, well I can only assume it was male, bent at the knees and grabbed my friend.

Jack Jackson, an unfortunate name and one he resented his father for giving him, my only friend in the world. And this thing, this horrible thing had taken him from me! Anger rose up inside me as I woke.

Crying, all I hear is crying. It's not me though. This time I'm not the one bawling. It's Mattie, my child. Almost a year old, she's a handful. I don't know how I deal with her, the product of a regretful one-night stand. Her father wants nothing to do with her. But that's just fine. I get my cheque once a month. And my darling Mattie is my saving grace. My muse. My reason for breathing. And now she's crying. I have to get to her.

I stumble over the blank easels. Finding my way through my maze of stuff to my tearful baby. I pick her up and soothe her. Her cot I haven't had time to put together is lying in its box against the wall. This constant moving is upsetting for a child so young, I know. But I don't stay in one place for long. I can't. It's too dangerous. I can't risk my child's life with the thing.

The thing…I don't know anything about it really, just that it's always in my dreams…I've heard stories though…it steals children, people really, when you look at him and he looks at you at the same time…there's been crude drawings…no concrete evidence…it has a multitude of names. Slender Man is the most common. I refer to it as the thing, because well it is the thing. The thing that set my world tumbling in around me when I was the tender age of ten. Mattie has stopped crying now. I place her back in her shambles of a pillow bed. Fast asleep once more, my darling looks angelic. Not a care in the world. How I wish I could be like her, unknowing of the world around me. Not having to constantly think of how to pay for necessities. What degrading thing I'll have to do today to put food on the table and a roof over our heads. I am her whole world. She knows only of what I show her.

How I would love to see the world through her eyes. Every day a brand new experience. An array of things she has never even seen lying all around her. And what must she think of me! The woman that looks after her, feeds her warm milk and mashed up banana. The woman who smiles whenever she looks at her. The woman who paints, well, half finishes paintings. That woman who picks her up and calls her Mattie, Darling or any name under the sun. That woman who comforts her when she screams. The woman who always has a distant look in her eyes, like she's constantly reliving past events.

Or maybe she thinks something much simpler. Her mother. Either way I love her, more than life itself. The only person I ever loved as much as her was Jack. And he was taken from me. I will do everything in my power to stop that from happening. I will not loose another to the Thing. Not in my lifetime, I promise.

Wide awake now, no chance of my falling back into my slumber. Might as well unpack a few things. As I always do, I start with my art supplies. I like surrounding myself in the scenes I create. However none of them are finished. Not a solitary one. If I ever even got close to completing one my subconscious is like 'Whoa hold up there, stop what your doing'. See I go into a kind of a trance when I'm painting; I'm never sure what I will paint. But every single time I finish a painting unbeknownst to myself I've painted a tall man with no face in the background wearing a pin-stripped suit. I never fully stopped thinking about the Thing. Always it was there, taunting me. And I just couldn't get over it. I never expected to either. Given this, I still hope that one day I'll be able to finish a painting or two and sell them. I've been told multiple times I have a gift with a paintbrush and that I should share it. But I can't. I will not subject anyone to the gruesome figure of the Thing. For all I know it may only take a picture for him to haunt you for always. That's not something I'm about to put the masses through. There's already too much heartache in the world, far too many sleepless nights for people. I can't and won't add to that. I refuse to add to the violence and destruction. Not I. There's no way I could live with my conscience after that. I'm finding it hard enough as it is. I could have, should have, done more to save Jack. Even if I had been taken too. I would have had a clear conscience. No, can't think like that. If I had, I never would have given birth to my wonderful beautiful Mattie.

I take my frustration out on the bubble wrap. Man, that stuff is fun. Jack and I spent hours bursting each individual bubble and then jumping on the rolls and rolls of it in his shed. His father made ornate furniture and shipped it overseas in crates. So there was always plenty of bubble wrap. We would get scolded for 'wasting' it, but we didn't care. At ten we didn't care about a whole lot. Except playing and joking. Oh, Jack, how I miss you. I'm so, so sorry you had to go. If you had stayed around maybe we would have got married like we planned. We'd have three kids, two boys and a girl. The girl would be the youngest so that she'd have two older brothers to protect her. We'd have a husky dog. We would live beside a lake and have a boat and a Volkswagen camper for weekend trips. We would take our kids around the country, showing them the wonders of this emerald isle. Sure we'd bicker like both of our sets of parents did, but it would be bliss. Darragh and Jack against the world.

As I snap out of my daydream I notice my cheeks are wet. This time I am the one crying. I can't help it. All those dreams never to be lived out. All because the Thing took him away from me. I wonder what happened to him...I've heard stories about the Thing keeping his victims as pets, creepy play things, but I refuse to believe this. Jack was just killed, he didn't suffer. The Thing probably feasted gruesomely on his flesh, savouring every juicy morsel, licking his lips. Oh wait...he doesn't have lips. How it happened doesn't matter. My Jack is dead. That I know for sure. Wondering how is not healthy. Neither is thinking about the why. I'm driving myself crazy.

I have to focus on my Mattie. My darling sweet Mattie that is waking up. I can tell as she has stopped muttering, she can hardly say a word but already she's a sleep talker. It'll only be a few minutes now till she's up and crying, wanting her breakfast and her nappy changed.

Five months later.

Yesterday was Mattie's birthday. Just me and her enjoying a bun with a candle. A very simple party. All her teddies were invited, but only a few turned up. She looked happy all the same. That's all I care about. Her happiness. I may not have got her anything big and fancy but I brought her away from the noisy city to the countryside. I've always loved the peace and quiet. You can actually see the stars at night, no glow of pollution. And during summer it's especially beautiful with the trees' luscious green plumage.

I haven't daydreamt about Jack over the past months. Sure, he's never far from my mind, but I've been focusing on my beautiful little girl and making life all I can for her. I managed to finish a painting. More than one even. With no tall, well-dressed man lurking ominously in the background. I have sold them too. Made a nice little profit for myself. That's what paid for this retreat. Our summer holiday beside the biggest beech forest in Europe. What an idyllic setting. It has given me great ideas for more paintings. I am going to give Mattie all the best things in life. No expense spared.

Such a lovely evening out. About nine-ish but the sun is still up. I want Mattie to see the sun setting over the lake. It's the longest day of the year so I should have time to trek through the two miles of forest between the B&B and the lake. It is truly a breathtaking sight. I want Mattie to see it. Even if she won't remember it when she's older.

I wrap her up in a hat and scarf, even though it's summer there's still a chill to the air. I don't want her getting ill. I shout into the owner that we're off and not to lock the door until we're back. And I set off. Mattie gurgles playfully in her pram. The path is too rough for it though. So I store it behind a large beech tree. I doubt anyone will take it, and even if someone does I have a spare one back in out apartment. I will have to paint some more when I get home though. A baby requires a lot of money. Oh but would you just look at her! Curled up in my arms, half asleep. The height of cuteness. One big ball of adorable. Her little button nose, butterfly of freckles. I just knew country air would be good for her. It brought out the red in her cheeks. She's glowing now, a real star. Oh how I adore everything about her.

I love her as much, if not more than I ever loved jack. Why does he keep popping into my head tonight…I suddenly feel very cold, I shiver. I can feel Mattie tense under me. My breathing gets rasped. My heart pounds against my ribcage. I hold Mattie tight for protection. I ready myself for an attack. I'm sure something is going to jump out of the shadows. I hear a rustle behind me, I spin around as quick as anything. I'm going to see my attackers face. Only thing is… I don't see anything. Oh hold on, over there, to the left, there's a squirrel or something. Just a woodland creature going about its business. Oh silly, silly me, I was petrified there. I realise I'm sweating, shivering and oh man, holding Mattie far too tight to my chest. She's whimpering, the poor pet. I pry her away from my bosom. I've a tissue in my back pocket I think, ah yes there it is. I wipe Mattie's nose. There, beautiful once more. She smiles at me and I keep walking.

Only about half a mile to the lake now, maybe less. I've never been good with distance. Direction I'm fine with, I'm quite good at it in fact. Jack always knew how far from home we were when we went on our grand adventures, and how long it would take to get back. Between us we needed no compass or map, no navigational equipment of any kind. Just Darragh and Jack against the world, the way we liked it. Nothing could stop us. Well…except the Thing. What is with me tonight!? I keep thinking about Jack. Wait…it's the 21st of June today…The Solstice.

I remember now. We were collecting sticks for a bonfire. Jack had the marshmallows in his back pocket. We were resting our toes in the stream. It was a scorching hot day. The sun was really splitting the stones. But the sky looked ominous. There was thunder in the air, black clouds on the horizon, but they didn't bother us. We were carefree ten-year-olds that had just built, in our eyes, the biggest bonfire this side of the Atlantic. We were well chuffed. It started to drizzle, nothing major. But Jack wanted to get a final few logs for our pile of spares that we had under a cover, before the rain got any heavier. I watched him run off to the edge of the woods just as the first roll of thunder swept around the clearing in an almighty BOOM.

Just at that moment I saw a dark looming silhouette. I tried to call out, to warn him but my voice was stuck in my throat. Fear prevented me from doing anything but cowering behind a rock. In that instant I knew what was going to happen. I was too terrified to do anything but clutch the rock as a form of comfort. Jack hadn't noticed the Thing. He calmly picked up a few sticks. Thunder and lightning didn't frighten him in the slightest, didn't scare me either back then. He turned to wave me over, must have found something interesting. Even from the distance he was away I could see the look of confusion in his face when he saw I wasn't where he left me. I wanted to do nothing more than jump up and make him run to me, anything to get him away from there. But I couldn't. To this day I can't explain it, but I just couldn't do anything but shake where I was crouched. At that moment Jack looked up at the Thing, as it looked at him and the Thing, Slender Man, Fear Dubh (Dark Man), whatever you want to call it, grabbed him. Just like that my Jack was gone. I sobbed into the rock. I howled all night until I was out of tears and my throat was raw. Racked with guilt and loss I couldn't find the strength to move. I wasn't found until the following evening. Everyone assumed there was a kidnapper who got Jack but hadn't seen me in my hiding place. It was a truth of sorts. I knew they'd never believe me; say it was my way of dealing with things. They sent out search parties, they didn't believe me that they'd never find him. They scoured the woods for days, weeks. He was gone forever. They didn't have any suspects. He was gone. No body, no one behind bars, no consolation for his grieving family. Just emptiness that he once filled.

It was this day, oh so many years ago that Jack was taken. About this time too. Christ…the forest is kind of eerie this time of evening…snap out of it Darragh. Maybe I should go back…I mean it's not as if Mattie would remember anyway. By the time I get there and start back to the B&B it'll be almost dark. I could trip and hurt Mattie. We could get lost. Yes, I think it's best to go back now. We've had long enough of a walk as it is. Better to be safe than sorry, that's for sure. And as an added bonus if we get back before nightfall the Thing will have had no chance to get Mattie. Not that he would…I'd lose everything if he did take her. I'd have nothing to live for. No, can't think like that. Got to get home. Wait…I don't remember there being a fallen tree covering the path. It looks old too, definitely did not just happen… oh god I took a wrong turn. Ms King, the owner of the B&B, did tell me these woods were tricky to navigate if you don't know them, especially at dusk. But I'm good at direction. OK, let me think, ok…if the sun is over there I should get back to the B&B if I go due west of here. Don't really want to leave the path though… Only thing is I've no idea how long I was walking in the wrong direction. This is bad, really, really bad. I need to get back. As soon as possible too. I don't feel good about being here, not tonight of all nights! Tomorrow would have been fine, perfect for a walk! But I couldn't wait, could I. What an idiot I am … if only…

The world runs on 'if onlys' and 'what ifs', doesn't it? I've got to get home. It's getting dark. I must have been walking for hours now. Well actually the sky looks kind of thunderous. It was clear a minute ago, I swear. Actually, where has the sun gone …it cannot be after eleven…can it? No, definitely not. It is not possible it's just stormy, that's it. Oh CRAP! Storms mean thunder and lightening and rain.

I've no rain gear. I'm completely unprepared. Stuff following the path. I can get us home much quicker. We need speed. I don't want to be out here any longer than absolutely necessary. So I'll head back. Due west. It'll all work out. OK go. It starts raining, light little bits. Damn it's getting heavier. It'll be pouring before long. I pick up the pace, jogging lightly. I hold Mattie close, don't want her getting wet and catching a cold. I sense the thunder looming. Any minute now we'll have a full lights show, complete with the orchestral music of the heavens. I've been ill at ease with storms ever since that faithful evening some twenty odd years ago.

I can hardly see now, the rain is coming down thick and fast, large droplets blinding my vision. I know I'm headed in the right direction though. I trip on a log, I didn't notice it. Ow…my ankle, I think it's broken. Where's Mattie? She slipped out of my arms when I fell, oh God. I can't see her. Wait, no, there she is. At the bottom of a tree lying beside a tall man in a suit. No, no, no, no, no, no, no. It CAN'T be. NOOOO! DON'T TAKE MY BABY. Mattie looks up at the tall, thin man as he looks at her. And he's gone, quick as a flash. My Mattie is with him. Gone. She's gone. My promise, ripped to shreds. I can't…I'm numb. He took my baby, my darling, my reason for living. Gone. All gone. Forever gone. Everything is gone. I stand up. My ankle is most probably broken. The physical pain of it is no match for the emotional pain of having my heart torn to shreds by this monster. The realisation. There's nothing left for me to live for. I stumble east. There's a motorway about two miles from here. I'll go there. I walk on. I'm numb. No feeling left in my unfortunately still beating heart. I'm already dead. I reach the motorway. I'm on a bridge.

You never know he might take a loved one from you some day. Maybe he'll take your reason for living like he did to me. I'm standing on the edge now. I jump. Falling fast, oh so fast. But the end doesn't come fast enough. I land right in front of a bus; rammed into the ground at 100kph. my body is no more. Lodged into the nooks and crannies of the front of the number 92 Wicklow-bound bus.

I see Jack holding Mattie. Slender man can't hurt me, not here. I'm free.

Injustice

By Siobhán Mulvey, age 17.

It comes. Starts burning, burning.
Flying up my throat,
stomach churning, churning.
Tears in my eyes
starts stinging, stinging.
Next thing I know I'm flying
you across the room.
That's what I'm thinking, thinking.
You should pay for all you've done.
Start breathing, breathing
all over again.

Rage unfurling, fists curling.
Want to scream, want to fall.
Wish I could do something, anything.
Break it all. Don't you dare
cover me; cover me
with a suffocating, suffocating
cloak of helplessness.
I want to throw you up.
Come at a better time. But
I can't even think
Body repulsing swallowing this
overwhelming smell of injustice.

It comes. Starts burning, burning.

And I'm wondering.

Slowly calming, calming.

Instinct withdrawing.

I'll fall. Falling.

Deep into a reassuring cloak of hopelessness.

Land softly,

smothering, smothering.

I will remember another time.

So please. Cover me, smother me, drown me

in absence of adrenaline firing

'Cause this earth is bubbling with injustice.

Bubbling. Slathering.

Waiting for someone to notice.

Try, try to reach.

But burning, burning,

hurling, hurling.

Covering, killing, oh so subtly.

Granny

By Siobhán Mulvey, age 17.

I remember you walking on the street
holding on to me tightly
your long overcoat heavy on your frame.

Scolding,
insulting without meaning to, yet
caring as much as one could.

Rosary beads
in your hands,
praying faithfully.

Don't fuss
or worry,
and don't quarrel.

Wrinkled face,
new teeth,
sharp in your gentle face.

Wise.
Remembering.
Reminiscing.

You didn't like taking tablets.
The nurses found them thrown in your handbag.
How we laughed.

I miss
you still,
almost all a dream.

First they said it was a burn,
then a rash,
then gangrene.

Amputate your leg
they did,
the stump covered up.

Only one leg.
It had spread to the other.
Only so much a person can take.
The last time I saw you
I said 'I love you.'
You said, rambling,

'Come down often.'
Yet we never got down
as much as we could.

Growing

By Hannah O'Boyle, age 16.

Sometimes I feel like a kid with adult problems.

Left with more questions than answers

and messes that even mothers can't fix.

Rational decisions that consider each consequence.

Everything is made within reason.

Responsible is what we must grow to be.

And still I long for my childhood.

The stolen moments that were lost among paperwork.

I still feel like a kid, with adult problems.

Mistaken Identity

By Aisling Rawle, age 15.

How does it feel knowing you're minutes away from meeting your idol? I imagine it's like a thirsty alcoholic walking into a bar. Me, personally? I think it's like God smiling down indulgently and saying, 'All right then. You deserve it.'

My hero is not a semi-talented singer or a good-looking actor, as is so common with other girls my age. My hero is Dr Simon O'Shea, a world-renowned scientist. His advances in physics have made him easily the most successful scientist in the country at present. I knew everything about him. He hates the colour brown. He started college at only sixteen – my age. He has a daughter who was supposed to have a mind as incredibly brilliant as his own. And in twenty minutes I was going to meet him.

I walked through the vast halls of the best university in the country in a dreamy state, on my way to his office. After a few persistent emails on my part, he had agreed to talk with me and gave me the time and place he would be when he finished his lecture.

The few people who were left in the building stared, probably wondering what a girl my age was doing there after 6pm. I was twenty minutes early. Feeling self-conscious, I found a room that wasn't locked where I could hide for a while. I closed the door and surveyed the room. It was very small, with only a naked bulb to illuminate the space. Mops, brushes, cloths and cleaning detergents were strewn haphazardly around. I took a deep, calming breath. I could smell dust, bleach and … smoke? Panic swept through me, and I whirled around, expecting to see a small fire. Instead, I met the eyes of a girl my age. She was sprawled on a chair, with her feet propped on another chair. She seemed relaxed, perfectly at ease, with a cigarette hanging from her lips.

'What are you doing in here?' I asked.

'No smoke alarm.' She gestured vaguely to the ceiling with a smirk.

'You're way too young to be smoking, never mind be in university' I accused. She opened her mouth to reply, but was interrupted by a sharp clicking on the other side of the door. She hastily dropped and stood on her cigarette. We both turned towards the door, waiting for it to open. It didn't. The only sound was the tapping and squeaking of retreating footsteps. The girl cursed. She walked over to the door and tried to open it. It wouldn't budge. She cursed again. 'He doesn't usually lock up until half six' she muttered. 'Better get comfortable. We might be here for a while.'

In my school – just as in all overly-expensive, private schools – there are two types of girls. The first type is the silly girl who is there because her father bought her way in. The other type is the focused, intelligent girl who worked her way there. I put myself in that category. I studied the girl in front of me, trying to determine which type she was. She was wearing black army boots and a yellow striped t-shirt and shorts. She had sandy blonde hair, dipped in pink and an exceptional amount of jewellery including countless bracelets and bangles. Whenever she moved, a merry jingling sound followed, like coins being shaken. Dark eyeliner ringed her eyes, giving her a gothic look. All these features of her appearance put together were strange, but more unsettling was her expression. Her lips were twisted slightly, as if repressing a smile. It was like she was in on some kind of joke that I didn't understand. Her eyes were dark orbs – taking everything in, revealing nothing.

She was neither the intelligent girl, nor the spoiled girl I concluded. Yes, she was that kind of girl. The one who doesn't mingle or take notes. The one who says nothing and does nothing, but seems to silently promise trouble.

I wanted to figure this girl out. 'Where do you go to school?' I asked politely.

'I dropped out of school,' she answered casually, as if commenting on the weather instead of admitting that she had damned her future.

'Your mother and father let you?' I asked incredulously.

'No mother. Just me and dad.'

'I'm sorry, that must be hard. By the way, it's "Dad and I",' I automatically corrected. She shot me a look that seemed much more amused than irritated.

'Well, he was … angry?' I asked curiously. She ran her hand through her hair nonchalantly and gave a humourless laugh. The merry tinkling from her jewellery and the cold laugh sounded so wrong together. Like wind chimes playing softly in a storm with dark skies.

'We argued about it every night. And then suddenly he just stopped arguing. Stopped caring. Now all he ever does is work. But that's nothing new.' She leaned forward in her chair and took a drag of her cigarette, a distant look on her face. 'He's my favourite person in the world, you know. He's kind of amazing. But he doesn't care about me anymore.' She gave the horrible laugh again. The only animated part of her was the smoke that leaked out of her lips. She stared at me with this cold, empty gaze. Her face was completely blank.

She shook her wrists. The sound seemed to alleviate some of the tension and her sarcastic expression was back. It guessed it was an expression most often worn by her.

'I take it you have a little more interest in your education,' she said dryly, eyeing my perfect, wrinkle free uniform. I rooted in my bag and confidently handed her my paper on Quantum Physics that I had planned to show Dr O'Shea. I had always imagined handing it to the highly-regarded scientist, and imagined him circulating it in awe to his peers. I was hoping that because of this paper, the next time I came to this university would be on a full scholarship. The girl took the pages and I watched smugly as her eyebrows shot up at the title. It was the first time I had seen her not looking completely bored. She flicked through the pages for a minute or two, before handing it back. 'You writ that?' She asked, sounding mildly impressed.

'I did,' I said proudly. 'By the way, it's "you wrote" that,' I corrected again. She showed me a pleasant smile and her middle finger.

I checked my watch. We had been locked in for nearly an hour. The girl was still a mystery to me, but I felt I had gained a little insight to her type. There was something about this girl I had yet to unveil, something that explained why she dropped out of school, and why her eyes were full of secrets. There was never silence in the small room thanks to the tinkling of the girl's jewellery and the creak of the chair as she swung back and forth on it. So I didn't notice when the door opened. I did, recognise, the sound of my idol's voice, so familiar to me from the internet.

'There you are,' Simon O'Shea said from the doorway with a key in his hand. I jumped up, delighted but shocked. He sounded so irritated.

'Sorry Dad, we got locked in.' My jaw dropped, and a wave of emotions washed over me. Shock, first and foremost. The girl was Marie O'Shea! How had I not recognised her dark eyes as her father's? And then, of course, embarrassment. Marie O'Shea was extraordinarily intelligent – and I had corrected her on her grammar. And finally – understanding. That was the reason behind all of her strange actions. No wonder she had dropped out of school. I was betting she knew everything. Well, knew everything she needed to become a genius scientist like her dad.

She was smirking beside her dad, as if she knew exactly what was going through my mind. 'Dad, this girl has a paper she was going to show you.' His face was blank for a moment, and then lit up with recognition. 'That's right. I'm sorry, it's quite late. Maybe I could look at it tomorrow?' After hearing Marie's story, I was no longer as interested in him as I was before. Instead, I met Marie's eyes. 'Yeah,' I agreed, 'tomorrow.' She grinned and her eyes glittered, reminding me of a star shooting across a dark, cloudless night. Dr. O'Shea said his goodbyes and left, and Marie, much more cheerfully, did the same. A moment later, her head popped back into the room. 'By the way,' she said, distorting her voice to mimic mine, 'page two of your paper is all wrong. Might want to check over some things before we meet again tomorrow.' And with a wink, the strange girl left, leaving both me, the 'smart girl' now feeling moronic, and a fading tinkling sound in the air.

Public Transport

By Deirdre Rawle, age 17.

Mr. Paul Paulson,   House No. 2,
Minister for Transport,   Left-of-the-Lamppost,
Dáil Éireann.   Forgotten on Shannon.

April 2002

Re: Lack of Public Transport, Forgotten on Shannon

Dear Mr. Paulson,

I'm writing with the intention of informing you about the serious lack of transportation in Forgotten on Shannon. My name is Joe and I am an unemployed lorry driver and current Chairperson of the Church Flower Society. There is not only a lack of public transport but also a lack of services for those who have their own means of transport.

While I appreciate the limited convenience of the communal village bicycle (known affectionately as 'Gertrude'), I'm sure you can understand the difficulty that arises in times such as bad weather or on occasions such as the Great Confusion of '92 (the day both Paddy AND Bridie wanted to cycle to the Post Office!) I hope you will confirm for me that there is something that can be done to accomplish the goal of making Forgotten on Shannon an easier place to live.

Forgotten on Shannon would undoubtedly be a beautiful place for tourists to visit: we have the most extensive selection of puddles in Ireland and when you are facing the wind the right way you can't even smell the slurry. I simply can't understand why there are no directions to our village on any of the nearby signposts! If there were to be a bus stop introduced to our town, I assure you there would be all sorts of celebrations. There might even be a mass to bless it followed by tea and sandwiches. How could you deny us such a thing? Having lived here for over fifty years I can tell you that in this small scenic town, the ratio of pubs to people is only slightly less impressive than our so-far unblemished record of drink driving incidents. Whether this is due to the general skill of our town's inhabitants or the fact that there is only one functioning vehicle and no petrol station for approximately seventy miles, I cannot be sure. I hope you understand how much the happiness of the locals would be increased by making Forgotten on Shannon a more accessible town.

To show you just how important this issue is (an issue might I add you have chosen to ignore or have somehow never been informed of. I suppose it could well be the latter, as people from Forgotten on Shannon seldom get out), I'm going to point out that according to Travel and Leisure magazine, our town has the single highest rate of BTDS ever recorded (i.e. Bored to Death Syndrome: a chronic mental illness caused by lack of facilities and / or transport). Symptoms include frequently stating the obvious and commenting on such things as the weather, X-Factor, obsessive adherence to the religious calendar and, in severe cases, the ability to form an original thought. Sufferers will inevitably die after falling into a Boredom Induced Coma (BIC).

Since all the young people left on foot, our death rate has risen by 73 per cent in the last ten years, with 98 per cent of those deaths being BTDS related. This is nothing short of an epidemic. As the nearest hospital is a thirty-five-day walk away, patients rarely make it. What would happen if finally a tourist were to stumble accidentally into our little village to find everybody dead? All I am suggesting to fix this disastrous problem is that one day a week a bus drives through the town in the morning and comes back again, at some point – just to let people see both a vehicle other than the local post van and a little bit of the world. I really think it would be a shame if you were to let our population die out. I'm leaving this fate in your hands. Lastly I would like to express my most insincere apologies for the date of this letter, as our postman is low on petrol and only makes a bi-annual venture outside of town. This letter may take some time to reach you. I hope it's not too late ...

Thank you for your time and consideration,

Joe McJoeson

Not such a bright life for Sunny

By Kate Reilly, age 17.

Making the appointment with a hooker and inviting her to meet me in the bar of a high class East Side Manhattan hotel was certainly something that was never specified in the job description. I didn't know what to expect. A short skirted, long-haired and conspicuous individual, bare legs crossed, cigarette dangling between be-taloned nails perhaps? As I hurried along the sidewalk, slightly late, I imagined judging sidelong glances been thrown and hushed, disapproving whispers being hissed about the lady waiting at the bar by the discreet and elite clientele enjoying their pre-lunch drinks. I expected a cool, calm, arrogant lady of the world. What I got, however, when I arrived at our point of rendezvous, was the one thing I didn't expect; a girl. Quite a young girl too. Attired in an unremarkable, plain, green dress, flat brown shoes and a mistrusting look in her wide eyes, I found that this pale waif was more disconcerting than the hussy with the red lipstick that I had in my mind. I nervously cleared my throat, shook a disinterested hand and quickly took out my recorder, lest the bar's occupants began to whisper about me as well. I had a list of questions prepared, and began with the basics; her name, age, where she came from, where she lives, where she works. I had begun my first interview with, to use the correct term, a prostitute.

'Sunny' (no more elaboration was given) is a nineteen-year-old orphan born and raised in New York City. She likes jazz music, the acting talents of Laurence Olivier and hotdogs. She also sells her body for money. The question I am mainly here to find out today is how does such a young girl get into this line of business? What circumstances must have prompted her to do so? Was it easy to do? And importantly, are there many young girls in the same position?

Sunny does not give away much. 'I never really had anyone to look out for me on the streets of New York. I was orphaned quite young. I lived off people in my neighbourhood until I was maybe twelve or thirteen, then I realised I couldn't do that forever.' I ask her what happened to her parents. She stares at the plush carpet for several minutes in silence. I am beginning to think she didn't hear my question when she whispers, 'They got sick.' She clears her throat. 'Our flat was damp. I mean steam would come off the walls on hot days and in the winter it was a pure icebox. They both smoked like trains, so I suppose their lungs wouldn't have been great anyway. They got sick, first my dad, then my mom. They coughed themselves to death.' She states this simply, as a matter of fact, while scuffing the carpet with the tip of her plimsoll. 'I couldn't really get any jobs, what with being so young and not very big. I was living on the streets at this stage, and the nights were getting cold.'

While she talks, she has a nervous habit of jiggling her foot up and down, something that gets worse when she talks about things you can tell she would probably rather not. 'I once knew this girl who was maybe five years older than me. She ran away from home 'cos of problems, and started earning her own money. I'd see her around town with nice coats on, getting into swanky cars and I wondered how she was doing it. I was desperate for my own way of making cash, you know? One day I was wandering around 5th Avenue looking at all the people Christmas shopping when I met her, hanging around with some fat, bald guy in a bad suit. She introduced me to him. His name was Maurice. Yeah. Her pimp.' She sighs, and I wonder what thoughts are going around in her head, whether this was the turning point in her seemingly bumpy road of life. 'Anyways, we talked for a while. I told her I was down on my luck. She didn't offer any help and I continued on my way. A week or two after that I bumped into Maurice. He was on his own. He recognised me, which surprised me. It was sorta flattering if you want to know the truth,' she shrugs. 'He offered me a place to stay for the night. I jumped at the chance, I mean it was that or half freeze to death again.'

At this point, I interrupt and offer her a cigarette. She declines, saying she doesn't smoke. Does she mind if I smoke then? 'Whatever,' comes the bored reply. I ask her to continue. 'So where was I? Oh yeah. Maurice. Little did I know he wasn't just being nice. I betcha it wasn't just an accident he bumped into me that day in New York either,' she reflects bitterly, her foot practically doing the

Highland Fling. 'He made me an offer I wasn't really in the position to refuse. He has quite a lucrative business. He keeps 5 or 6 of us, his 'employees', in whatever establishment he's working in at the moment. Might be a elevator guy in a hotel with weary traveller types wall to wall, might be a busboy in a restaurant full of lonely businessmen, might be a coat check guy in a club, ready to jump on the drunkest of them. Maurice knows what he's doing.'

'What are the going rates per night?'

'Whatever Maurice decides. If he thinks the guy looks quite dumb he'll charge him double. Same if he's smaller than Maurice. He can be quite dirty when he wants to be. I mean if you get a guy who's agreed to pay five dollars a go, and he pays his five dollars, Maurice'll say he wants ten. He'll say ten was the deal. The guy will eventually pay ten cause Maurice is quite dirty when he wants to be. It's how business is done.' She glances around her, looking enviously at the fur coats and huge brooches milling around the bar. I enquire about the target market. What kind of people come to Maurice to tipper the sting of loneliness? Surely the lowest of the low, those who have no morals, no dignity left to lose? At this question, Sunny laughs. Well, almost. 'Oh, people you wouldn't believe. Any one of these swanky people you see in here, any of those smart professors in the university, any of the hotshot business guys in their fancy cars, they all come to Maurice in the evenings. I just expected the scum of the earth the first few weeks in the job, but you get all kinds. All kinds.'

I ask Sunny if she has any regrets about getting into this line of work. It is hardly what can be defined as the dream career. She shrugs. I get the feeling of a spirit resigned to their fate. 'One girl that worked for Maurice some time ago, I mean this is before I started, she wanted to get outta the game. She walked away from Maurice. He begged her to stay, got quite angry according to the others. None of the girls ever saw her again. She just disappeared. I don't want to disappear,' Sunny says quietly and I get the sense that 'disappear' is code for something else. I ask Sunny what she spends her money on. 'Oh, mansions and fancy cars obviously,' she says with no hint of sarcasm, staring coolly into my eyes. I try to hold her stare but those large blue eyes win and I avert my gaze. 'Clothes.

Food. Shoes. Whatever the hell else I need to live. I'm not anyone's mistress; I'm a one-night memory to be forgotten. I don't get showered with dresses and fur-trimmed gloves. I work like anybody else in this city, just so I don't die.'

'A fairly bleak outlook on life, no?'

'I guess,' she shrugs. 'It's just the truth, though.'

Based on the character of Sunny from The Catcher in the Rye.

Endless

By Eve Tansey, age 12.

In the maze. I don't know how I got here, but it doesn't matter. I have to stay focused. Focused on escaping and staying alive. Duke runs towards me. It's scary how quickly I forgot about him. He's whimpering at me. He's favouring his front left leg. I examine him closer. There's a thorn in his paw. I remove it quickly. Duke licks it a few times before, apparently satisfied, he runs off to explore further.

He is by my side again within minutes. We're both sprinting now. I can tell something's wrong. We are being chased by… Who? … What? I'm not paying attention. I trip and fall. Duke stands over me, growling. He protects me as long as he can. I watch him being kicked aside. It is the last thing I see before the world goes black.

I wake up alone. Well, not quite alone. Duke is curled up in the corner, not moving. I stand up stiffly. I am in a small, dark, musty room. I cross the room and kneel beside Duke. He is barely breathing. A sharp pain shoots through my head. I can feel the dried blood on the back of my hair. I stroke Duke's fur before examining my surroundings. There is a tap in the corner. I turn it on. The water is stale and warm but I gulp it down regardless.

The door, surprisingly, is unlocked. I glance back at Duke, promising myself that I would come back for him. I walk out. It looks like a shack. I do not know how else to describe it. 'Finally, you wake up,' I say, grinning. Duke is standing up in the doorway, his head cocked to one side. I look through the pages left on a desk in the corner. However, none of them make any sense. The ramblings of a madman. Among them, I discover a ball of black string and an old key.

After filling a bottle of water, we leave the shack. It appears to be centred in the middle of the maze. I pick a path at random and start to walk. Duke barks at me. He is standing next to one of the other paths. I decide to trust his judgement and follow him. I unwind the ball of string behind me as I walk. After twenty minutes or so of walking, I come to a halt. The ground in front of me is crisscrossed with black string. I quickly realise that we have been going around in circles. I retrace our steps and walk in a different direction.

I have a strange feeling that we are being watched. Duke starts to growl. In the corner of my eye, I see a shadow getting closer. We break into a run. Some time later, we come to a stone wall with an old wooden door. It appears to be locked. I take out the key and fit it into the old, rusty lock. The creature is coming. Coming closer and closer. It's gaining on us fast. I can hear its heavy breathing. I can smell its wet fur. I risk a look at the beast. It is a mix between a man and an animal. I stand still for a moment, transfixed. I wait too long. The beast reaches us and with a roar, lunges at me.

I scramble backwards. There is nowhere else to run. It is standing over me. Duke attacks the creature's leg. The beast flings him away. He lies crumpled at my feet. I come to my senses and struggle to open the door. Using all my remaining strength, I haul Duke through after me and slam the door. Breathing heavily, I stare at the door as if it might open again. When it does not, I turn to Duke. He wags his tail feebly and licks my hand. Duke and I turn towards home.

I feel something warm and wet at my feet. I open my eyes to the familiar surroundings of my bedroom. My loyal companion is lying on the end of my bed, licking my toes. A chewed up puzzle book just beside him, still open at the maze puzzle I had been doing before I fell asleep.

Day Tripping

By The Response Project, age 15-18.

Like a seed on shallow ground
waiting for the roots to grow
Unaware danger's close.
So far to go.

A child is born in the twenty-first century.
Its imagination grows,
but in the wrong family.

Day tripping.
Ticket in her pocket.
Day tripping.
Loved ones in her pocket.

The girl grows up.
Unhappy and alone.
Wants to run away.
But can't on her own.

Tired and cold.
Living on a train.
Travelling miles
and miles everyday.

Day tripping.
Ticket in her pocket.
Day tripping.
Loved ones in her pocket.

Red dress
Across the platform.
Turns around.
Dazzling smile.

Reflection in the window.
Turns around and just knows.
She's running out of time tonight.

This could be the
last dance.
This could be her
last chance.
It's gonna be a
night tonight.

www.ingramcontent.com/pod-product-compliance
Lightning Source LLC
Chambersburg PA
CBHW061455170626
46811CB00004B/1518